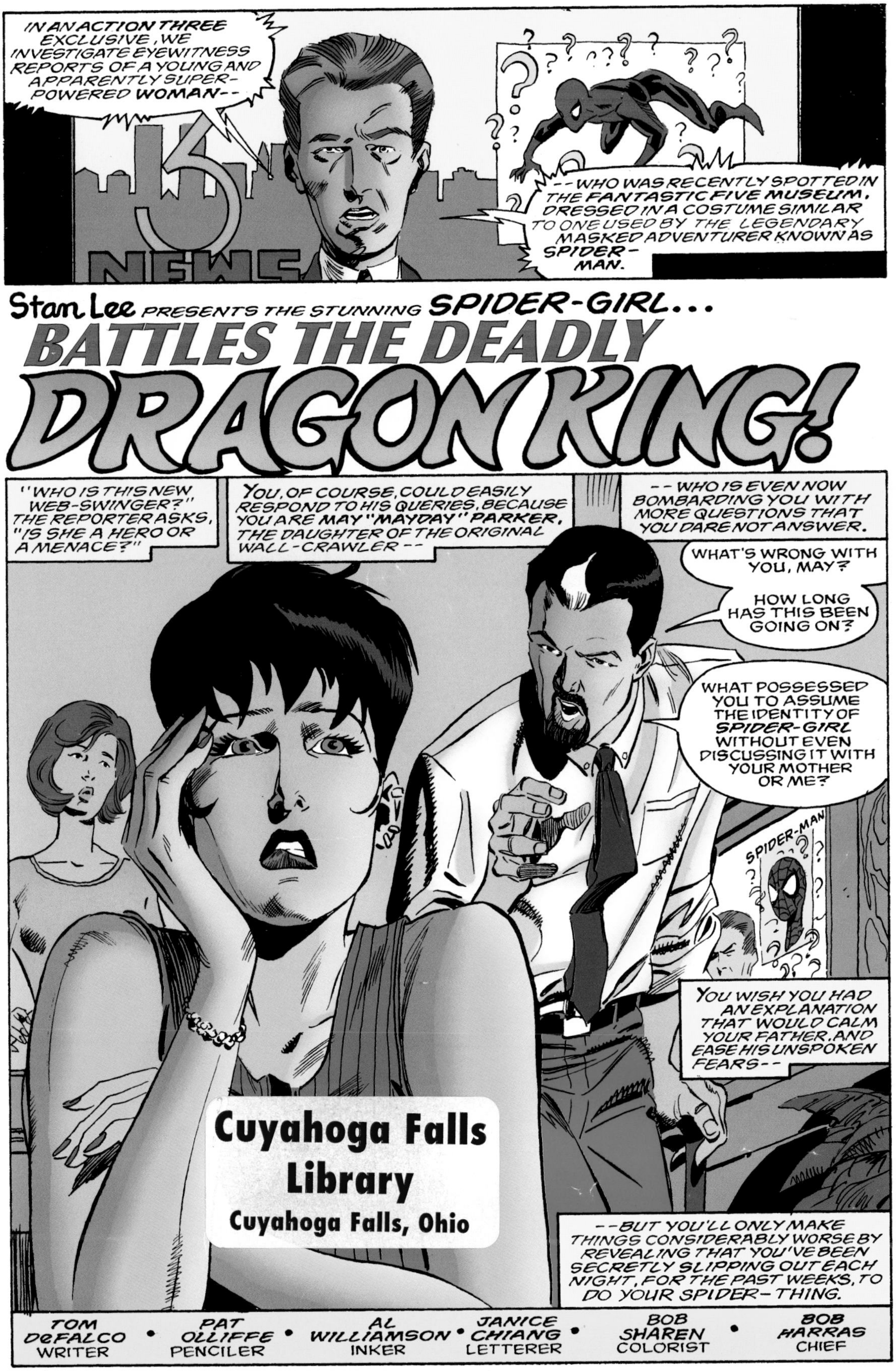
IN AN ACTION THREE EXCLUSIVE, WE INVESTIGATE EYEWITNESS REPORTS OF A YOUNG AND APPARENTLY SUPER-POWERED WOMAN--
--WHO WAS RECENTLY SPOTTED IN THE FANTASTIC FIVE MUSEUM, DRESSED IN A COSTUME SIMILAR TO ONE USED BY THE LEGENDARY MASKED ADVENTURER KNOWN AS SPIDER-MAN.
NEWS
Stan Lee PRESENTS THE STUNNING SPIDER-GIRL...
BATTLES THE DEADLY
DRAGON KING!
"WHO IS THIS NEW WEB-SWINGER?" THE REPORTER ASKS, "IS SHE A HERO OR A MENACE?"
YOU, OF COURSE, COULD EASILY RESPOND TO HIS QUERIES, BECAUSE YOU ARE MAY "MAYDAY" PARKER, THE DAUGHTER OF THE ORIGINAL WALL-CRAWLER--
--WHO IS EVEN NOW BOMBARDING YOU WITH MORE QUESTIONS THAT YOU DARE NOT ANSWER.
WHAT'S WRONG WITH YOU, MAY?
HOW LONG HAS THIS BEEN GOING ON?
WHAT POSSESSED YOU TO ASSUME THE IDENTITY OF SPIDER-GIRL WITHOUT EVEN DISCUSSING IT WITH YOUR MOTHER OR ME?
SPIDER-MAN
YOU WISH YOU HAD AN EXPLANATION THAT WOULD CALM YOUR FATHER AND EASE HIS UNSPOKEN FEARS--
--BUT YOU'LL ONLY MAKE THINGS CONSIDERABLY WORSE BY REVEALING THAT YOU'VE BEEN SECRETLY SLIPPING OUT EACH NIGHT, FOR THE PAST WEEKS, TO DO YOUR SPIDER-THING.
TOM DeFALCO WRITER • PAT OLLIFFE PENCILER • AL WILLIAMSON INKER • JANICE CHIANG LETTERER • BOB SHAREN COLORIST • BOB HARRAS CHIEF

VISIT US AT

www.abdopub.com

Spotlight, a division of ABDO Publishing Company Inc., is the school and library distributor of the Marvel Entertainment books.

Library bound edition © 2006

Library of Congress Cataloging-in-Publication Data

Battles the Deadly Dragon King!

ISBN 1-59961-025-6 (Reinforced Library Bound Edition)

All Spotlight books are reinforced library binding
and manufactured in the United States of America

Spotlight

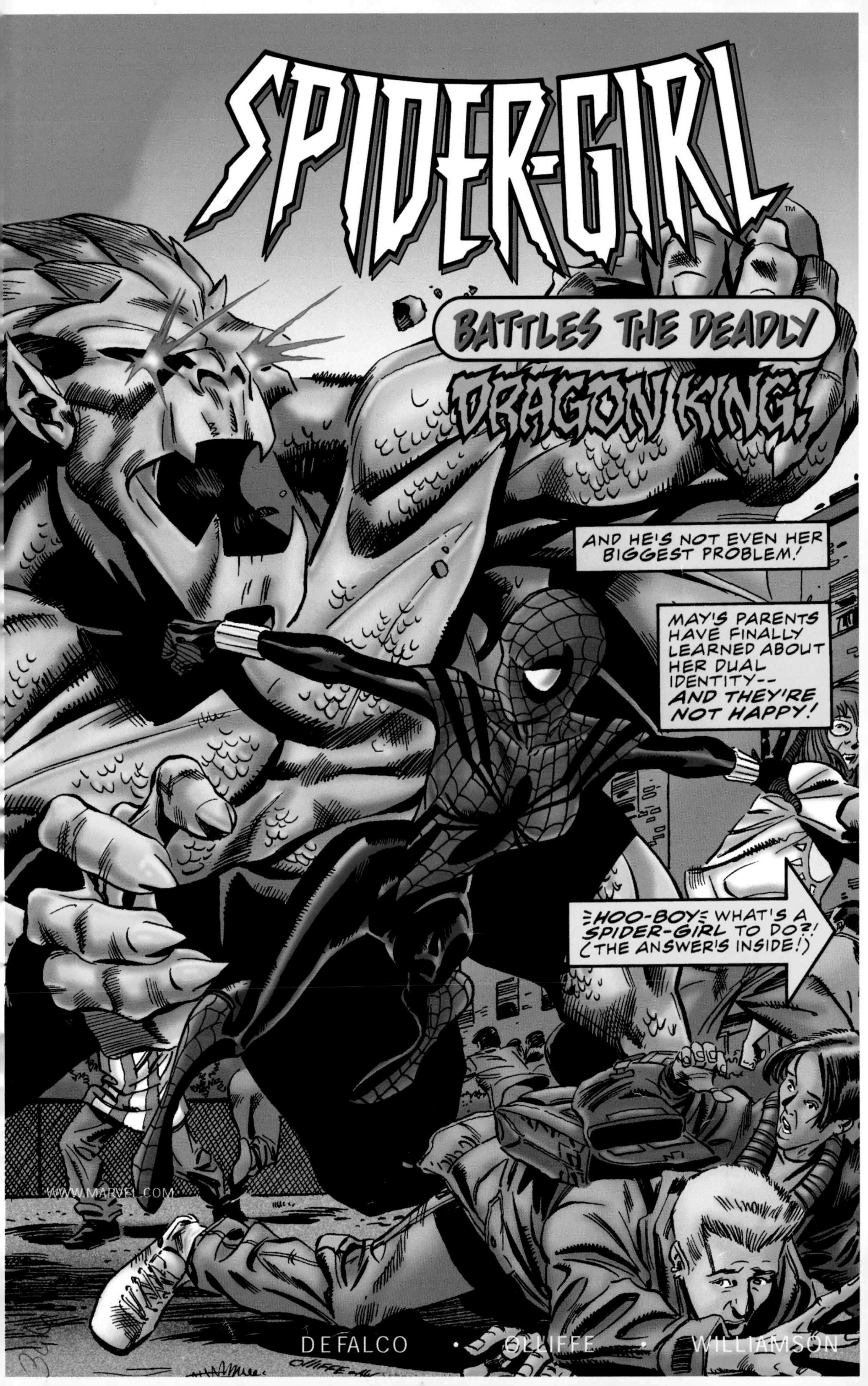
SPIDER-GIRL™
BATTLES THE DEADLY
DRAGON KING!™
AND HE'S NOT EVEN HER BIGGEST PROBLEM!
MAY'S PARENTS HAVE FINALLY LEARNED ABOUT HER DUAL IDENTITY-- AND THEY'RE NOT HAPPY!
HOO-BOY! WHAT'S A SPIDER-GIRL TO DO?! (THE ANSWER'S INSIDE!)
WWW.MARVEL.COM
DEFALCO • OLLIFFE • WILLIAMSON

DON'T TUNE ME OUT, YOUNG LADY!

I...I'M NOT IGNORING YOU, DADDY...I-IT'S JUST THAT I...*uhhhh...*

YOU THINK BEING A *SUPER HERO* IS SOME KIND OF *GAME?*

IT COST ME A *LEG* AND ALMOST MY *LIFE!*

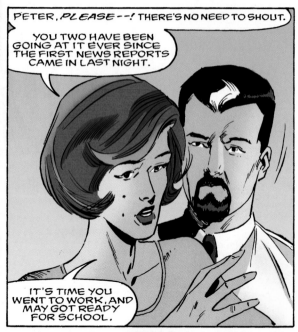

PETER, *PLEASE* --! THERE'S NO NEED TO SHOUT.

YOU TWO HAVE BEEN GOING AT IT EVER SINCE THE FIRST NEWS REPORTS CAME IN LAST NIGHT.

IT'S TIME YOU WENT TO WORK, AND MAY GOT READY FOR SCHOOL.

MAYBE YOU'RE RIGHT, MARY JANE.

WE DO NEED A BREAK FROM EACH OTHER.

BUT I INTEND TO FINISH THIS CONVERSATION WHEN I GET HOME.

THANKS FOR STEPPING IN, MOM.

THE WAY HE WAS ROLLING, I THOUGHT WE'D BE STUCK HERE ALL DAY.

DO YOU BLAME HIM FOR BEING SO UPSET--?!

YOU ACTED VERY *IRRESPONSIBLY!*

HEY! IT'S NOT LIKE I'M DOING ANYTHING THAT *HE* WASN'T AT MY AGE!

THE SITUATION WAS TOTALLY DIFFERENT!

HE HAD A GOOD REASON TO BECOME *SPIDER-MAN.*

RIGHT! RIGHT! AND I'M JUST A LITTLE GIRL PLAYING DRESS-UP!

I SHOULD HAVE KNOWN YOU'D TAKE HIS SIDE!

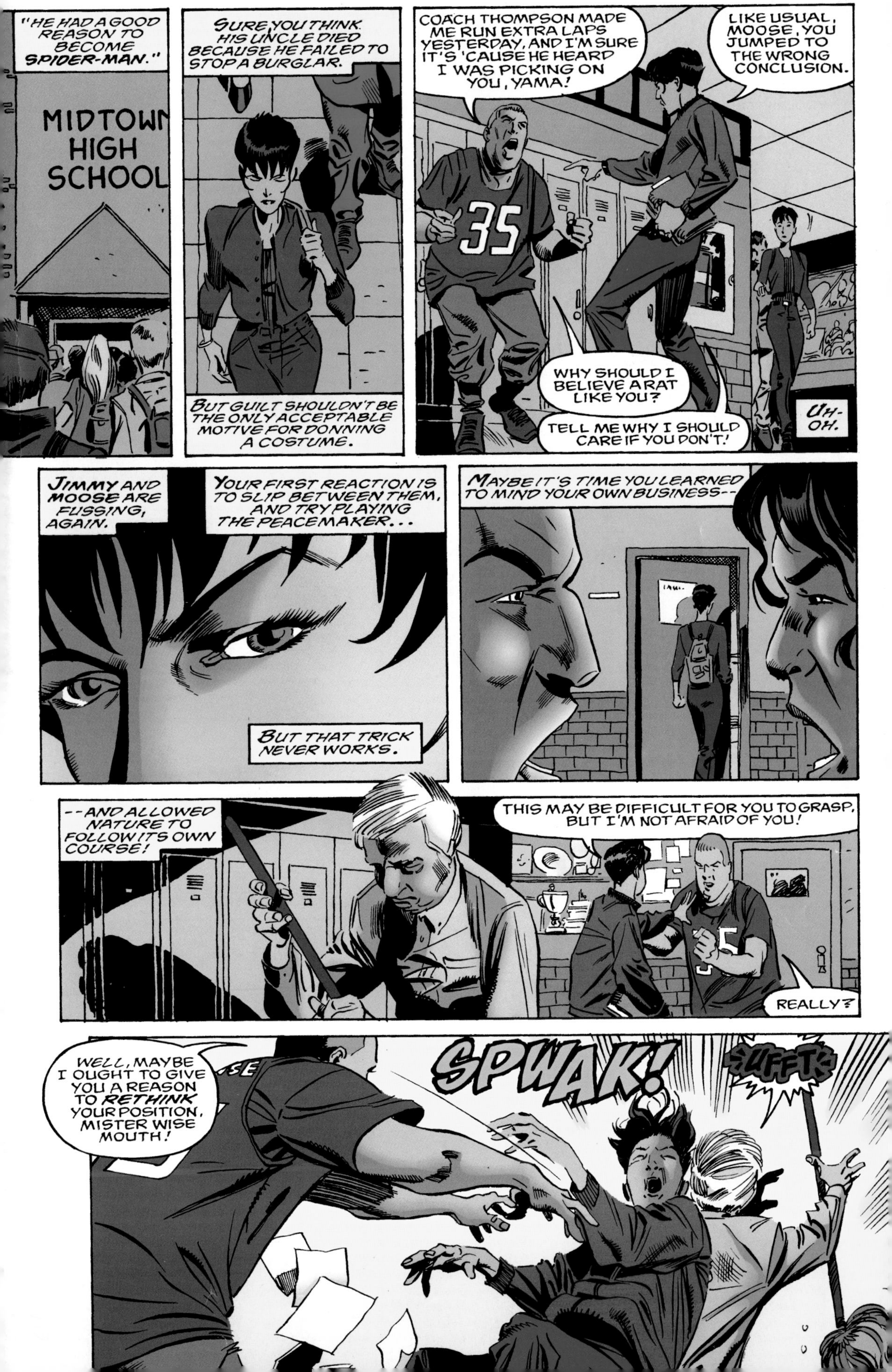
"HE HAD A GOOD REASON TO BECOME SPIDER-MAN."
MIDTOWN HIGH SCHOOL
SURE, YOU THINK HIS UNCLE DIED BECAUSE HE FAILED TO STOP A BURGLAR.
BUT GUILT SHOULDN'T BE THE ONLY ACCEPTABLE MOTIVE FOR DONNING A COSTUME.
COACH THOMPSON MADE ME RUN EXTRA LAPS YESTERDAY, AND I'M SURE IT'S 'CAUSE HE HEARD I WAS PICKING ON YOU, YAMA!
LIKE USUAL, MOOSE, YOU JUMPED TO THE WRONG CONCLUSION.
WHY SHOULD I BELIEVE A RAT LIKE YOU?
TELL ME WHY I SHOULD CARE IF YOU DON'T!
UH-OH.
JIMMY AND MOOSE ARE FUSSING, AGAIN.
YOUR FIRST REACTION IS TO SLIP BETWEEN THEM, AND TRY PLAYING THE PEACEMAKER...
BUT THAT TRICK NEVER WORKS.
MAYBE IT'S TIME YOU LEARNED TO MIND YOUR OWN BUSINESS--
--AND ALLOWED NATURE TO FOLLOW ITS OWN COURSE!
THIS MAY BE DIFFICULT FOR YOU TO GRASP, BUT I'M NOT AFRAID OF YOU!
REALLY?
WELL, MAYBE I OUGHT TO GIVE YOU A REASON TO RETHINK YOUR POSITION, MISTER WISE MOUTH!
SPWAK!
UFFT!

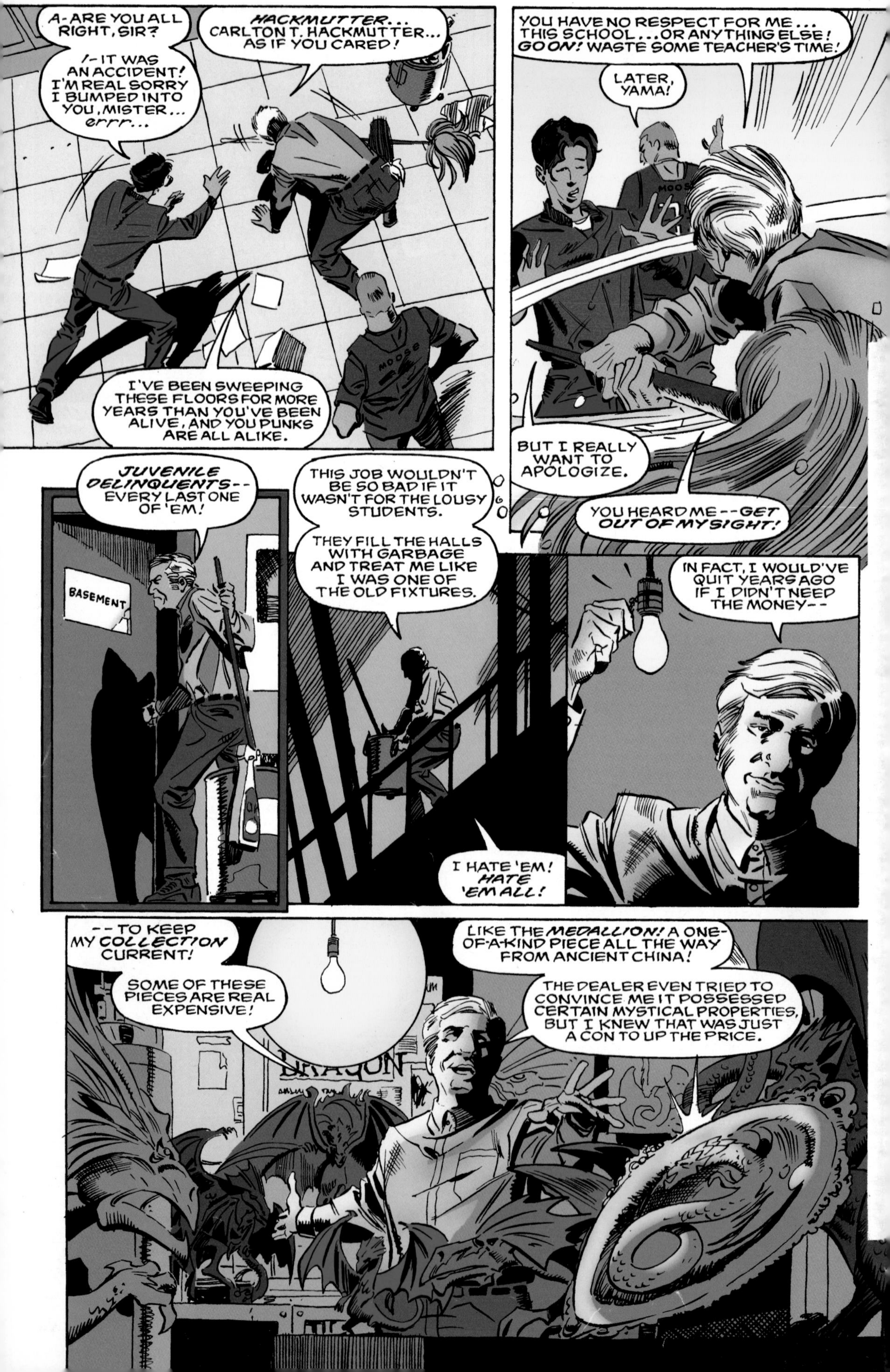
A-ARE YOU ALL RIGHT, SIR?
I-IT WAS AN ACCIDENT! I'M REAL SORRY I BUMPED INTO YOU, MISTER... errr...
HACKMUTTER... CARLTON T. HACKMUTTER... AS IF YOU CARED!
I'VE BEEN SWEEPING THESE FLOORS FOR MORE YEARS THAN YOU'VE BEEN ALIVE, AND YOU PUNKS ARE ALL ALIKE.
MOOSE
YOU HAVE NO RESPECT FOR ME... THIS SCHOOL... OR ANYTHING ELSE! GO ON! WASTE SOME TEACHER'S TIME!
LATER, YAMA!
MOOSE
BUT I REALLY WANT TO APOLOGIZE.
YOU HEARD ME--GET OUT OF MY SIGHT!
JUVENILE DELINQUENTS--EVERY LAST ONE OF 'EM!
BASEMENT
THIS JOB WOULDN'T BE SO BAD IF IT WASN'T FOR THE LOUSY STUDENTS.
THEY FILL THE HALLS WITH GARBAGE AND TREAT ME LIKE I WAS ONE OF THE OLD FIXTURES.
IN FACT, I WOULD'VE QUIT YEARS AGO IF I DIDN'T NEED THE MONEY--
I HATE 'EM! HATE 'EM ALL!
--TO KEEP MY COLLECTION CURRENT!
SOME OF THESE PIECES ARE REAL EXPENSIVE!
LIKE THE MEDALLION! A ONE-OF-A-KIND PIECE ALL THE WAY FROM ANCIENT CHINA!
THE DEALER EVEN TRIED TO CONVINCE ME IT POSSESSED CERTAIN MYSTICAL PROPERTIES, BUT I KNEW THAT WAS JUST A CON TO UP THE PRICE.

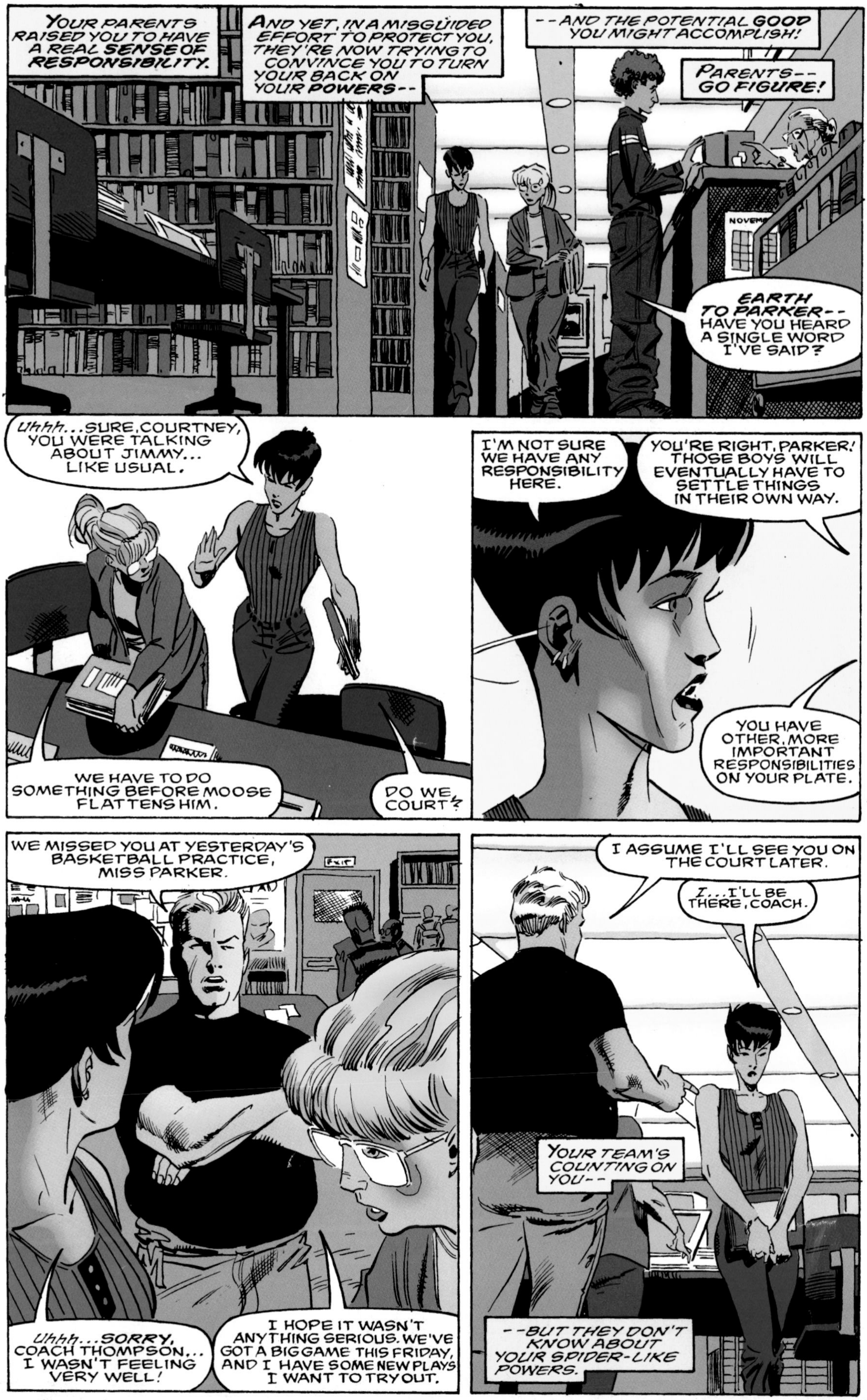
YOUR PARENTS RAISED YOU TO HAVE A REAL SENSE OF RESPONSIBILITY.
AND YET, IN A MISGUIDED EFFORT TO PROTECT YOU, THEY'RE NOW TRYING TO CONVINCE YOU TO TURN YOUR BACK ON YOUR POWERS--
--AND THE POTENTIAL GOOD YOU MIGHT ACCOMPLISH!
PARENTS-- GO FIGURE!
EARTH TO PARKER-- HAVE YOU HEARD A SINGLE WORD I'VE SAID?
UHHH... SURE, COURTNEY, YOU WERE TALKING ABOUT JIMMY... LIKE USUAL.
WE HAVE TO DO SOMETHING BEFORE MOOSE FLATTENS HIM.
DO WE, COURT?
I'M NOT SURE WE HAVE ANY RESPONSIBILITY HERE.
YOU'RE RIGHT, PARKER! THOSE BOYS WILL EVENTUALLY HAVE TO SETTLE THINGS IN THEIR OWN WAY.
YOU HAVE OTHER, MORE IMPORTANT RESPONSIBILITIES ON YOUR PLATE.
WE MISSED YOU AT YESTERDAY'S BASKETBALL PRACTICE, MISS PARKER.
UHHH... SORRY, COACH THOMPSON... I WASN'T FEELING VERY WELL!
I HOPE IT WASN'T ANYTHING SERIOUS. WE'VE GOT A BIG GAME THIS FRIDAY, AND I HAVE SOME NEW PLAYS I WANT TO TRY OUT.
I ASSUME I'LL SEE YOU ON THE COURT LATER.
I... I'LL BE THERE, COACH.
YOUR TEAM'S COUNTING ON YOU--
--BUT THEY DON'T KNOW ABOUT YOUR SPIDER-LIKE POWERS.

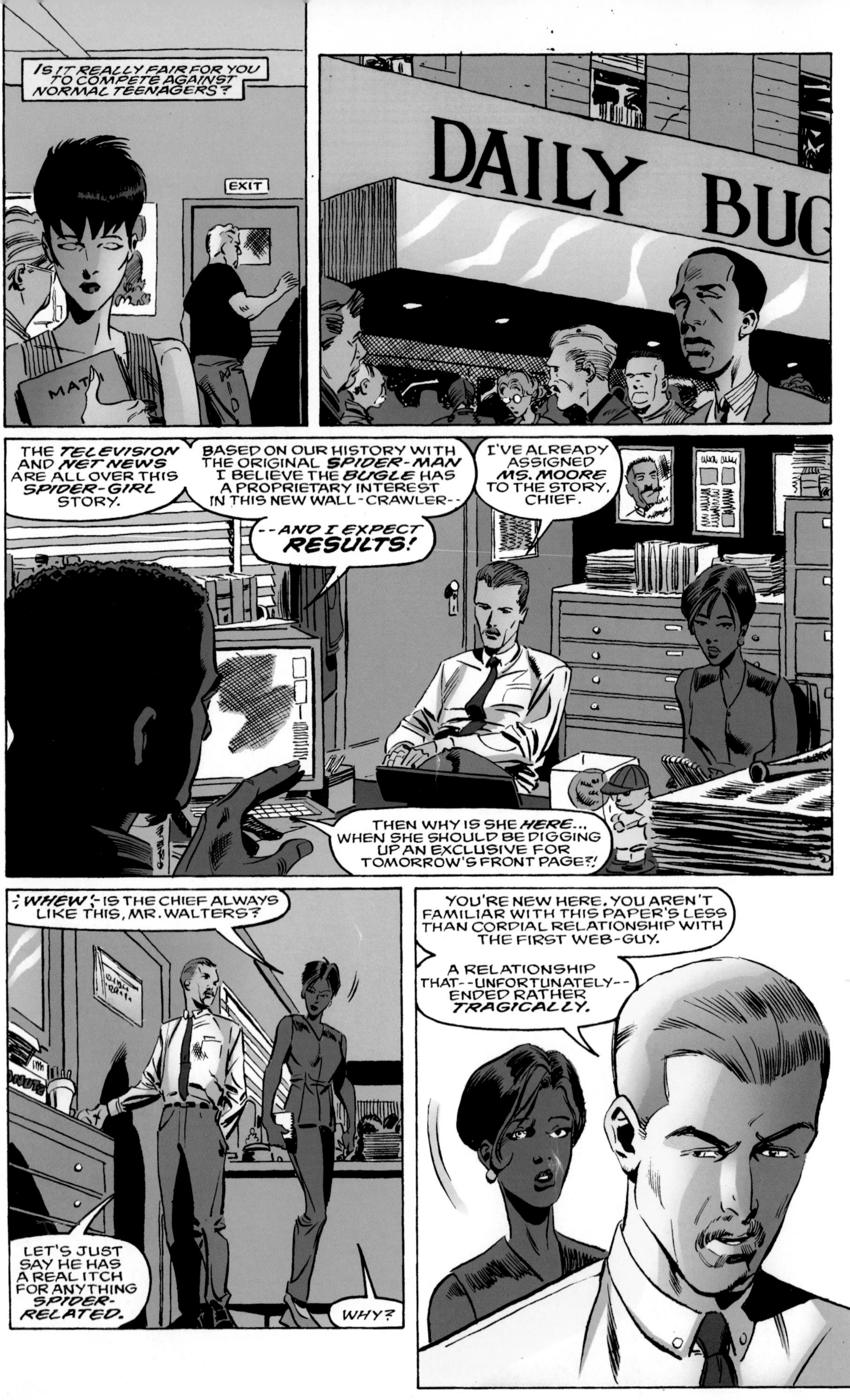
IS IT REALLY FAIR FOR YOU TO COMPETE AGAINST NORMAL TEENAGERS?
EXIT
MATH
DAILY BUG
THE TELEVISION AND NET NEWS ARE ALL OVER THIS SPIDER-GIRL STORY.
BASED ON OUR HISTORY WITH THE ORIGINAL SPIDER-MAN I BELIEVE THE BUGLE HAS A PROPRIETARY INTEREST IN THIS NEW WALL-CRAWLER--
--AND I EXPECT RESULTS!
I'VE ALREADY ASSIGNED MS. MOORE TO THE STORY, CHIEF.
THEN WHY IS SHE HERE... WHEN SHE SHOULD BE DIGGING UP AN EXCLUSIVE FOR TOMORROW'S FRONT PAGE?!
-WHEW- IS THE CHIEF ALWAYS LIKE THIS, MR. WALTERS?
LET'S JUST SAY HE HAS A REAL ITCH FOR ANYTHING SPIDER-RELATED.
WHY?
YOU'RE NEW HERE. YOU AREN'T FAMILIAR WITH THIS PAPER'S LESS THAN CORDIAL RELATIONSHIP WITH THE FIRST WEB-GUY.
A RELATIONSHIP THAT--UNFORTUNATELY--ENDED RATHER TRAGICALLY.

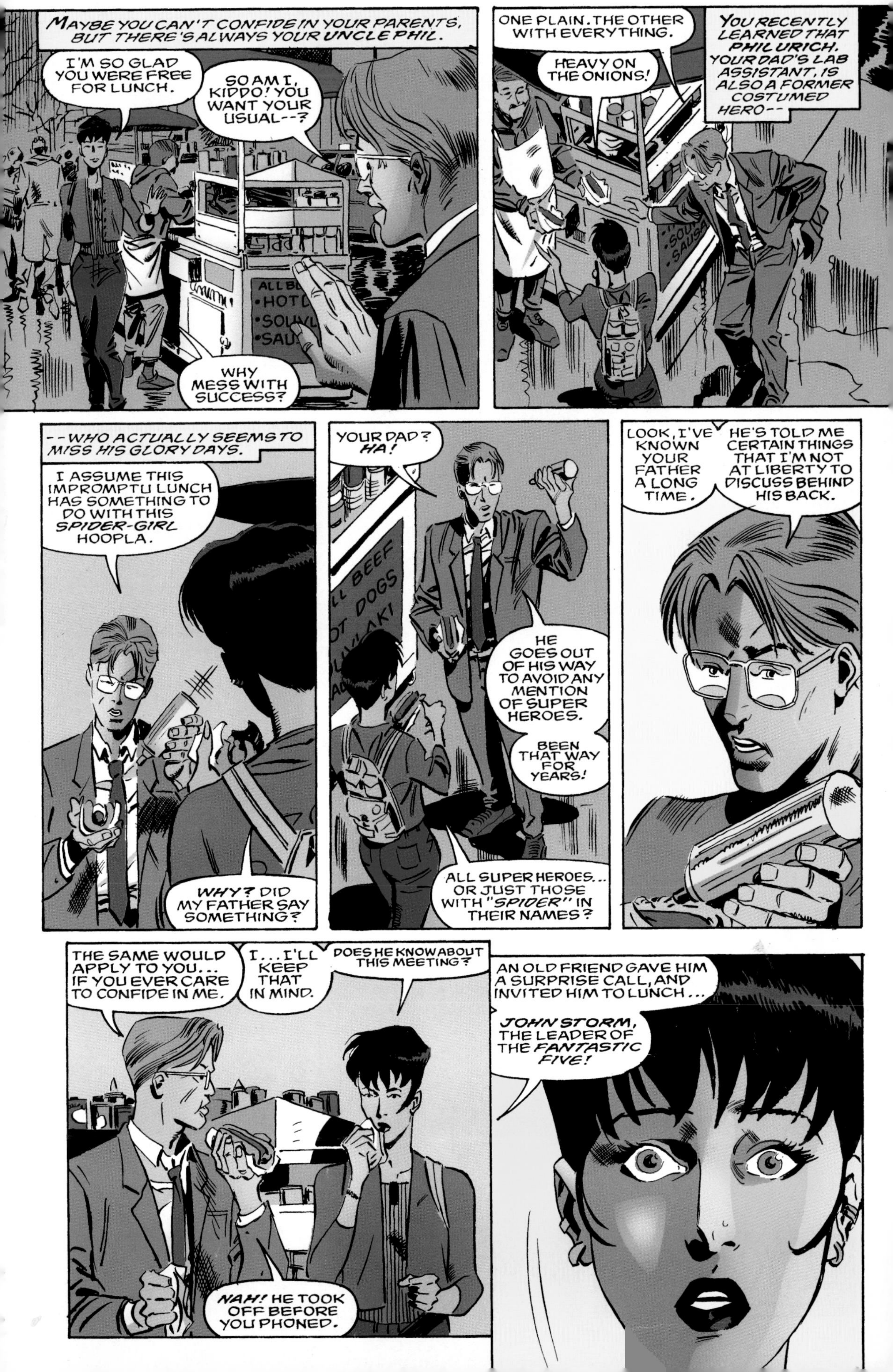
MAYBE YOU CAN'T CONFIDE IN YOUR PARENTS, BUT THERE'S ALWAYS YOUR UNCLE PHIL.
I'M SO GLAD YOU WERE FREE FOR LUNCH.
SO AM I, KIDDO! YOU WANT YOUR USUAL--?
WHY MESS WITH SUCCESS?
ALL BE
HOT D
SOUVL
SAUS
ONE PLAIN. THE OTHER WITH EVERYTHING.
HEAVY ON THE ONIONS!
YOU RECENTLY LEARNED THAT PHIL URICH, YOUR DAD'S LAB ASSISTANT, IS ALSO A FORMER COSTUMED HERO--
--WHO ACTUALLY SEEMS TO MISS HIS GLORY DAYS.
I ASSUME THIS IMPROMPTU LUNCH HAS SOMETHING TO DO WITH THIS SPIDER-GIRL HOOPLA.
WHY? DID MY FATHER SAY SOMETHING?
YOUR DAD? HA!
HE GOES OUT OF HIS WAY TO AVOID ANY MENTION OF SUPER HEROES.
BEEN THAT WAY FOR YEARS!
ALL SUPER HEROES... OR JUST THOSE WITH "SPIDER" IN THEIR NAMES?
LOOK, I'VE KNOWN YOUR FATHER A LONG TIME.
HE'S TOLD ME CERTAIN THINGS THAT I'M NOT AT LIBERTY TO DISCUSS BEHIND HIS BACK.
THE SAME WOULD APPLY TO YOU... IF YOU EVER CARE TO CONFIDE IN ME.
I... I'LL KEEP THAT IN MIND.
DOES HE KNOW ABOUT THIS MEETING?
NAH! HE TOOK OFF BEFORE YOU PHONED.
AN OLD FRIEND GAVE HIM A SURPRISE CALL, AND INVITED HIM TO LUNCH...
JOHN STORM, THE LEADER OF THE FANTASTIC FIVE!

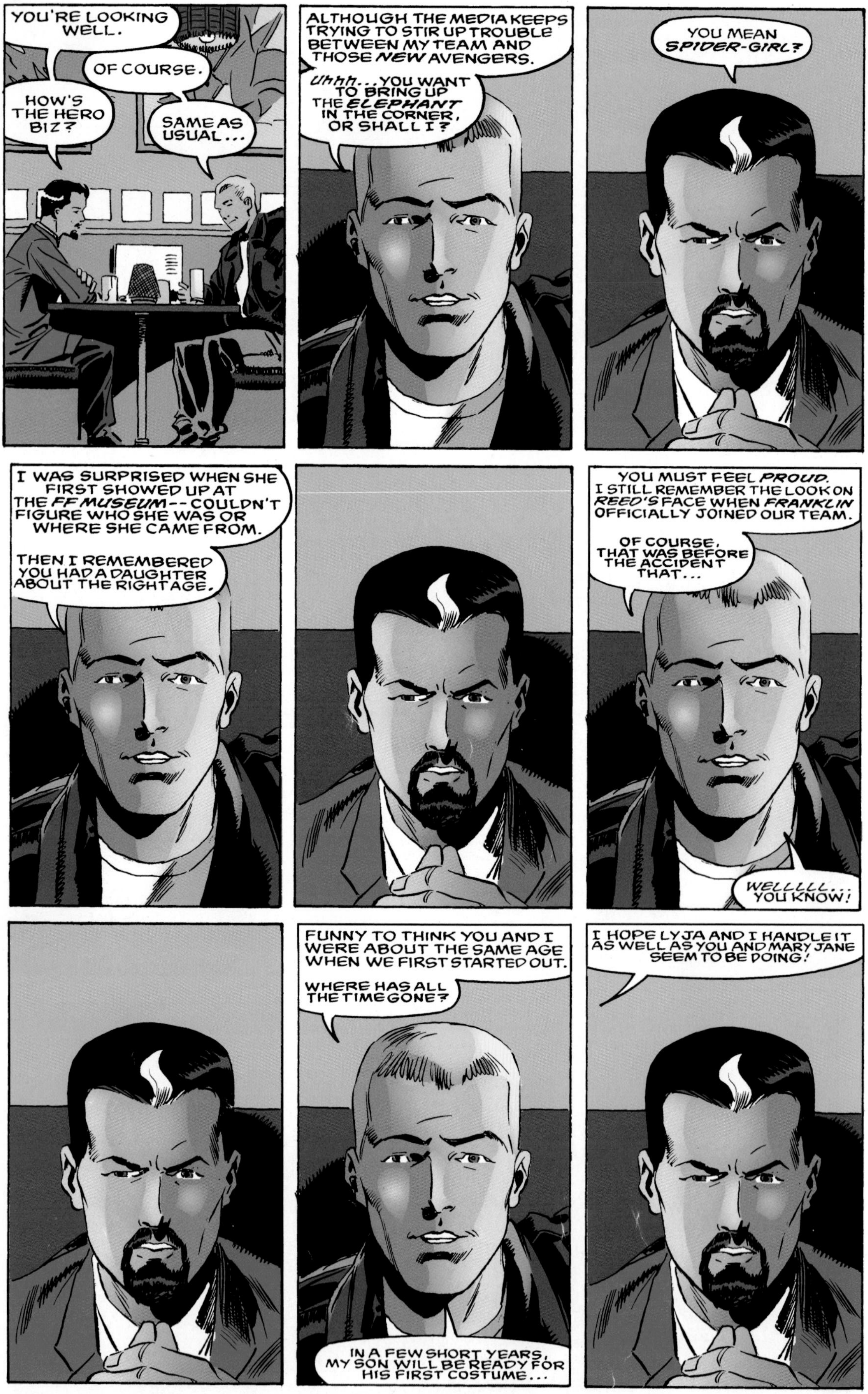
YOU'RE LOOKING WELL.
OF COURSE.
HOW'S THE HERO BIZ?
SAME AS USUAL...
ALTHOUGH THE MEDIA KEEPS TRYING TO STIR UP TROUBLE BETWEEN MY TEAM AND THOSE NEW AVENGERS.
Uhhh... YOU WANT TO BRING UP THE ELEPHANT IN THE CORNER, OR SHALL I?
YOU MEAN SPIDER-GIRL?
I WAS SURPRISED WHEN SHE FIRST SHOWED UP AT THE FF MUSEUM--COULDN'T FIGURE WHO SHE WAS OR WHERE SHE CAME FROM.
THEN I REMEMBERED YOU HAD A DAUGHTER ABOUT THE RIGHT AGE.
YOU MUST FEEL PROUD. I STILL REMEMBER THE LOOK ON REED'S FACE WHEN FRANKLIN OFFICIALLY JOINED OUR TEAM.
OF COURSE, THAT WAS BEFORE THE ACCIDENT THAT...
WELLLLL... YOU KNOW!
FUNNY TO THINK YOU AND I WERE ABOUT THE SAME AGE WHEN WE FIRST STARTED OUT.
WHERE HAS ALL THE TIME GONE?
IN A FEW SHORT YEARS, MY SON WILL BE READY FOR HIS FIRST COSTUME...
I HOPE LYJA AND I HANDLE IT AS WELL AS YOU AND MARY JANE SEEM TO BE DOING!

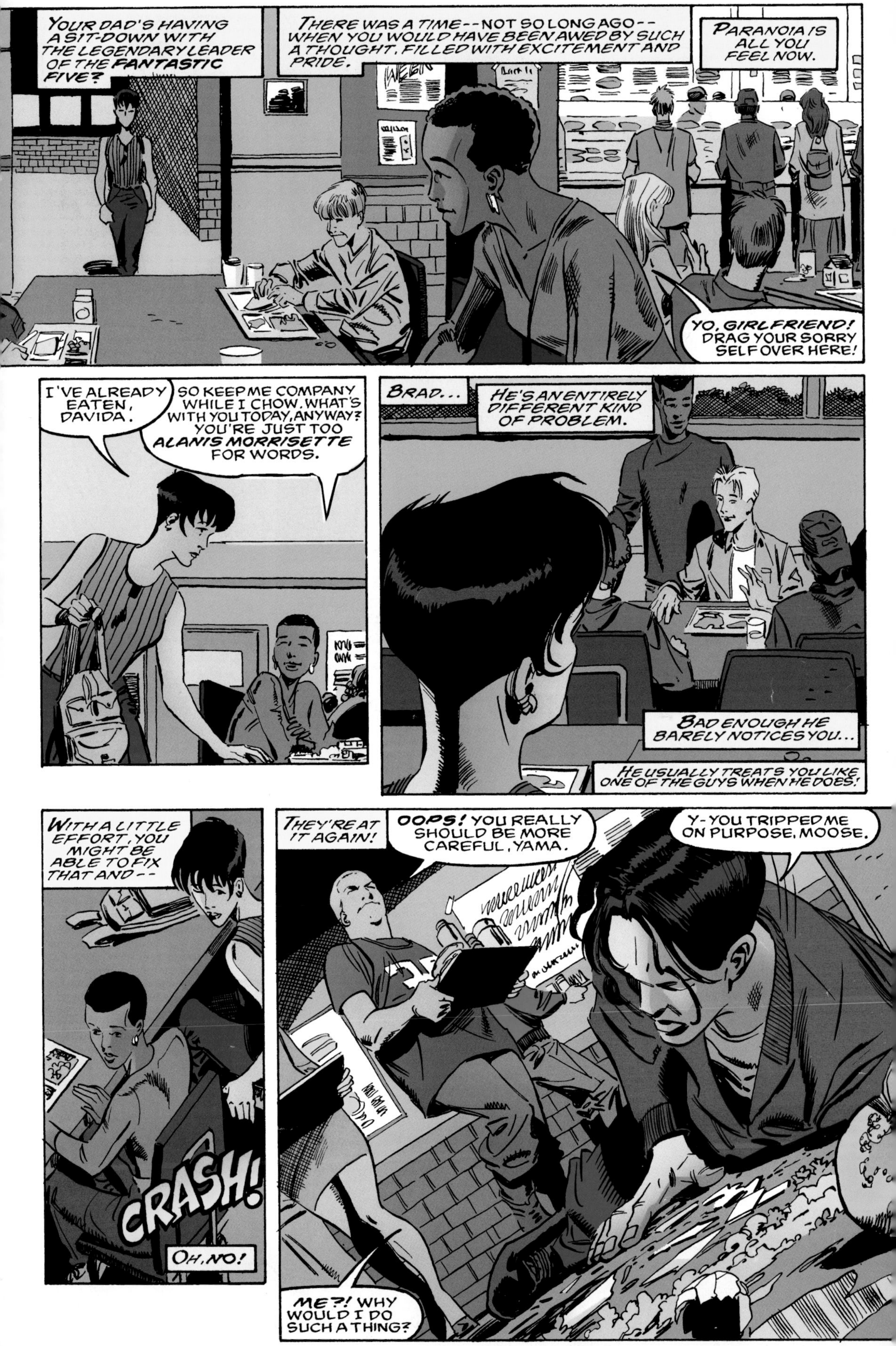

YOUR DAD'S HAVING A SIT-DOWN WITH THE LEGENDARY LEADER OF THE FANTASTIC FIVE?
THERE WAS A TIME--NOT SO LONG AGO--WHEN YOU WOULD HAVE BEEN AWED BY SUCH A THOUGHT. FILLED WITH EXCITEMENT AND PRIDE.
PARANOIA IS ALL YOU FEEL NOW.
YO, GIRLFRIEND! DRAG YOUR SORRY SELF OVER HERE!
I'VE ALREADY EATEN, DAVIDA.
SO KEEP ME COMPANY WHILE I CHOW. WHAT'S WITH YOU TODAY, ANYWAY? YOU'RE JUST TOO ALANIS MORRISETTE FOR WORDS.
BRAD...
HE'S AN ENTIRELY DIFFERENT KIND OF PROBLEM.
BAD ENOUGH HE BARELY NOTICES YOU...
HE USUALLY TREATS YOU LIKE ONE OF THE GUYS WHEN HE DOES!
WITH A LITTLE EFFORT, YOU MIGHT BE ABLE TO FIX THAT AND--
CRASH!
OH, NO!
THEY'RE AT IT AGAIN!
OOPS! YOU REALLY SHOULD BE MORE CAREFUL, YAMA.
Y-YOU TRIPPED ME ON PURPOSE, MOOSE.
ME?! WHY WOULD I DO SUCH A THING?

DON'T PLAY INNOCENT WITH ME, YOU MISANTHROPIC MORON!

YOU REALLY SHOULD LEARN TO RELAX, YAMA. *STRESS KILLS!*

WHAT'S THE PROBLEM HERE, GENTLEMEN?

I WISH I KNEW, SIR. YOUNG MISTER YAMA SEEMS RATHER AGITATED AND I'VE BEEN TRYING TO HELP HIM.

REALLY, MANSFIELD? I NEVER REALIZED YOU WERE SUCH A CARING INDIVIDUAL.

STAY AWAY FROM EACH OTHER FOR THE REST OF THE DAY, OR YOU'LL BOTH JOIN ME FOR DETENTION.

MISERABLE PUNKS!

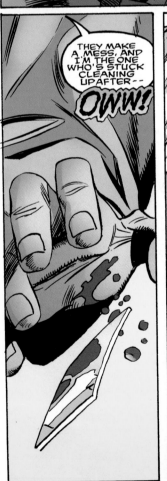

THEY MAKE A MESS, AND I'M THE ONE WHO'S STUCK CLEANING UP AFTER-- *OWW!*

GREAT! *JUST GREAT!*

OHMIGOSH! IT LOOKS LIKE MR. HACKMUTTER CUT HIMSELF--!

HACKMUTTER-- THE JANITOR!

MISTER *WHO*--?

Y-YOU KNOW THAT OLD COOT'S NAME?

DON'T YOU--?

GOOD FOR NOTHING SMART-MOUTHED WISE GUYS!

I COULD BLEED TO DEATH FOR ALL THEY CARE!

AND THE DOGGONED TEACHERS AIN'T MUCH BETTER!

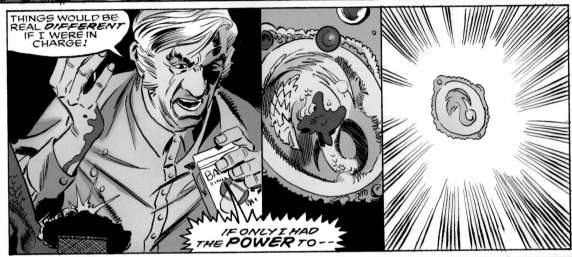

THINGS WOULD BE REAL *DIFFERENT* IF I WERE IN CHARGE!

IF ONLY I HAD THE **POWER** TO--

Uh-oh!

S-SOMETHING'S HAPPENING TO ME!

SOMETHING STRANGE--

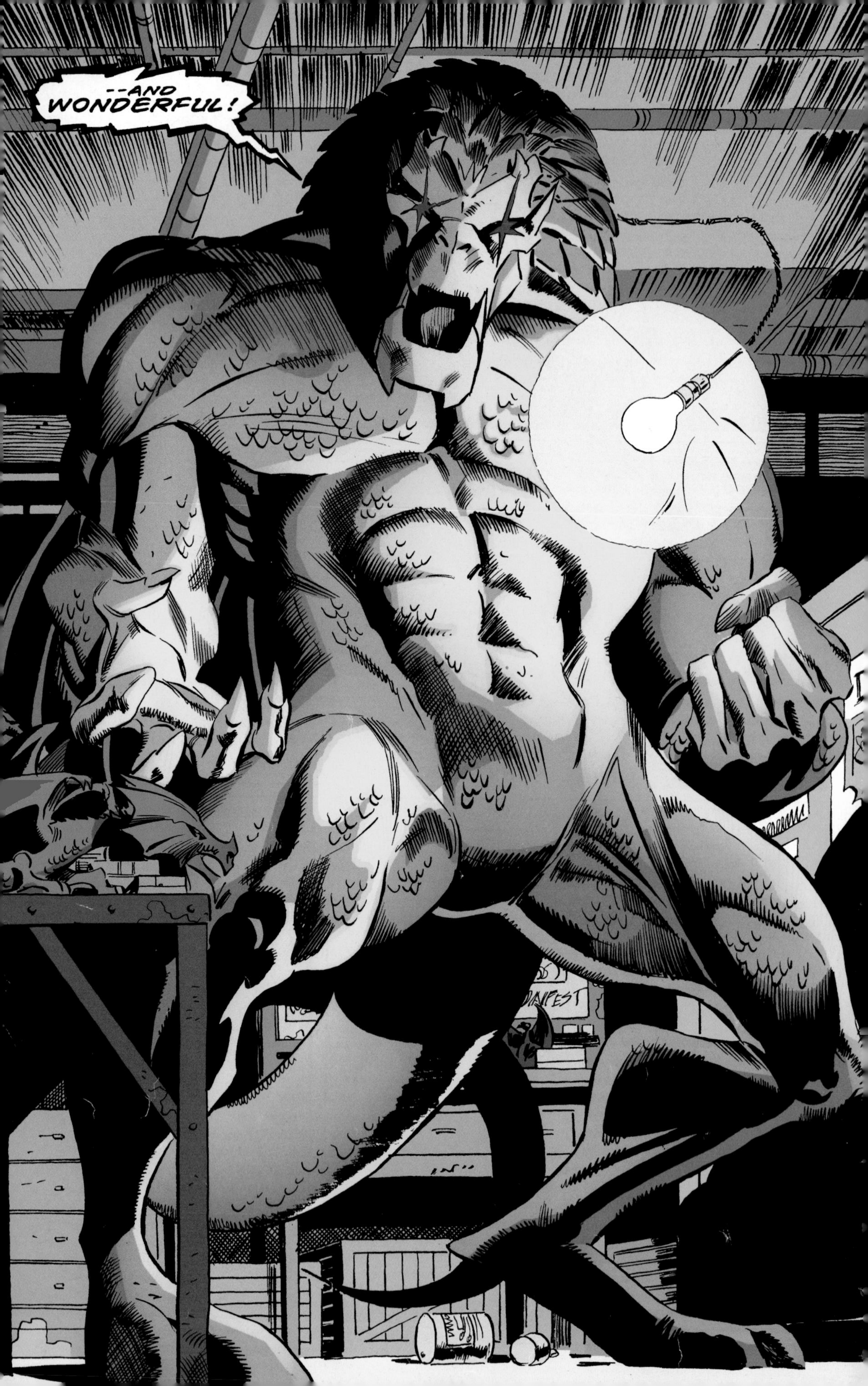
--AND WONDERFUL!

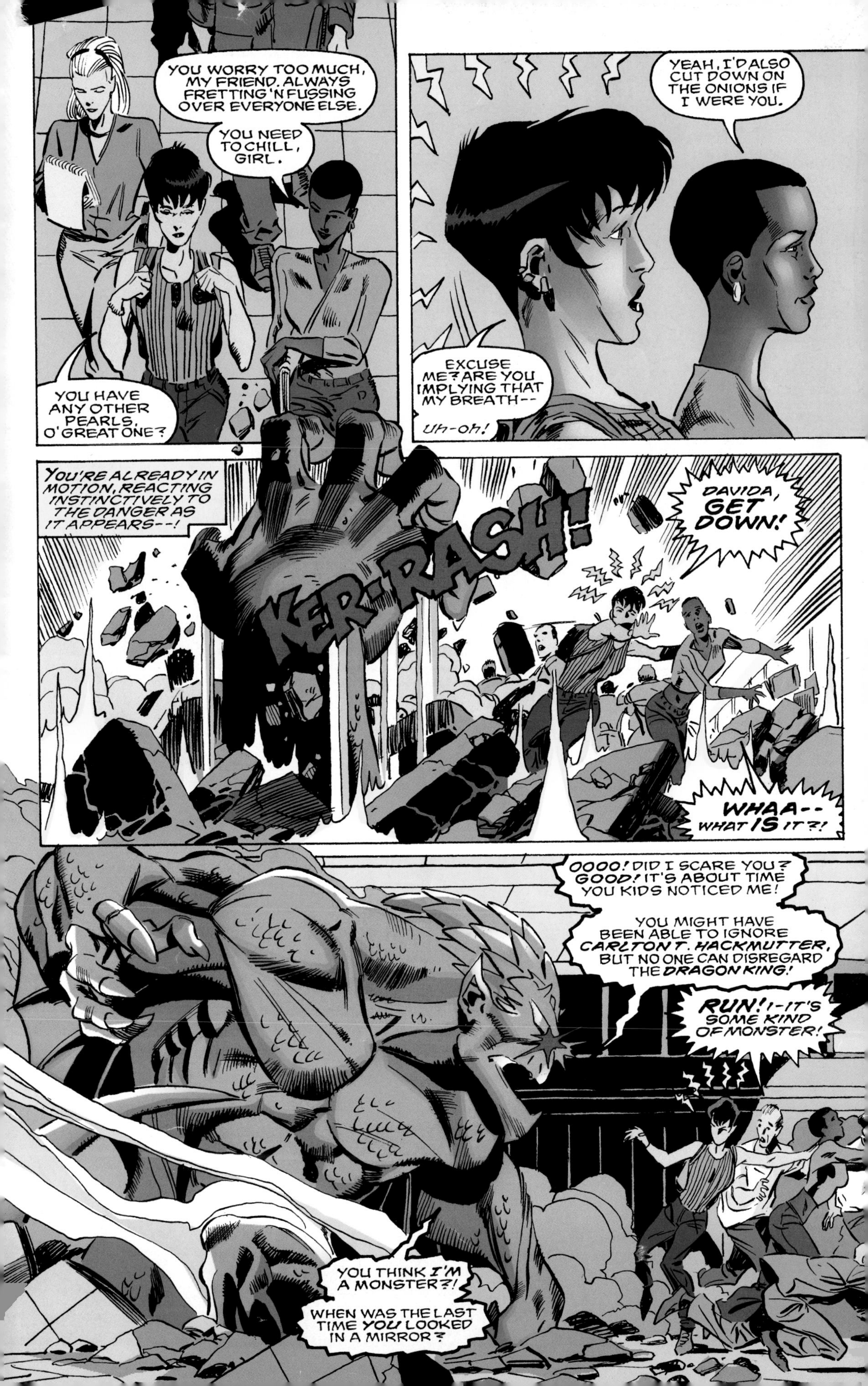
YOU WORRY TOO MUCH, MY FRIEND. ALWAYS FRETTING 'N FUSSING OVER EVERYONE ELSE.
YOU NEED TO CHILL, GIRL.
YOU HAVE ANY OTHER PEARLS, O' GREAT ONE?
YEAH, I'D ALSO CUT DOWN ON THE ONIONS IF I WERE YOU.
EXCUSE ME? ARE YOU IMPLYING THAT MY BREATH--
Uh-oh!
YOU'RE ALREADY IN MOTION, REACTING INSTINCTIVELY TO THE DANGER AS IT APPEARS--!
KER-RASH!
DAVIDA, GET DOWN!
WHAA-- WHAT IS IT?!
OOOO! DID I SCARE YOU? GOOD! IT'S ABOUT TIME YOU KIDS NOTICED ME!
YOU MIGHT HAVE BEEN ABLE TO IGNORE CARLTON T. HACKMUTTER, BUT NO ONE CAN DISREGARD THE DRAGON KING!
RUN! I-IT'S SOME KIND OF MONSTER!
YOU THINK I'M A MONSTER?!
WHEN WAS THE LAST TIME YOU LOOKED IN A MIRROR?

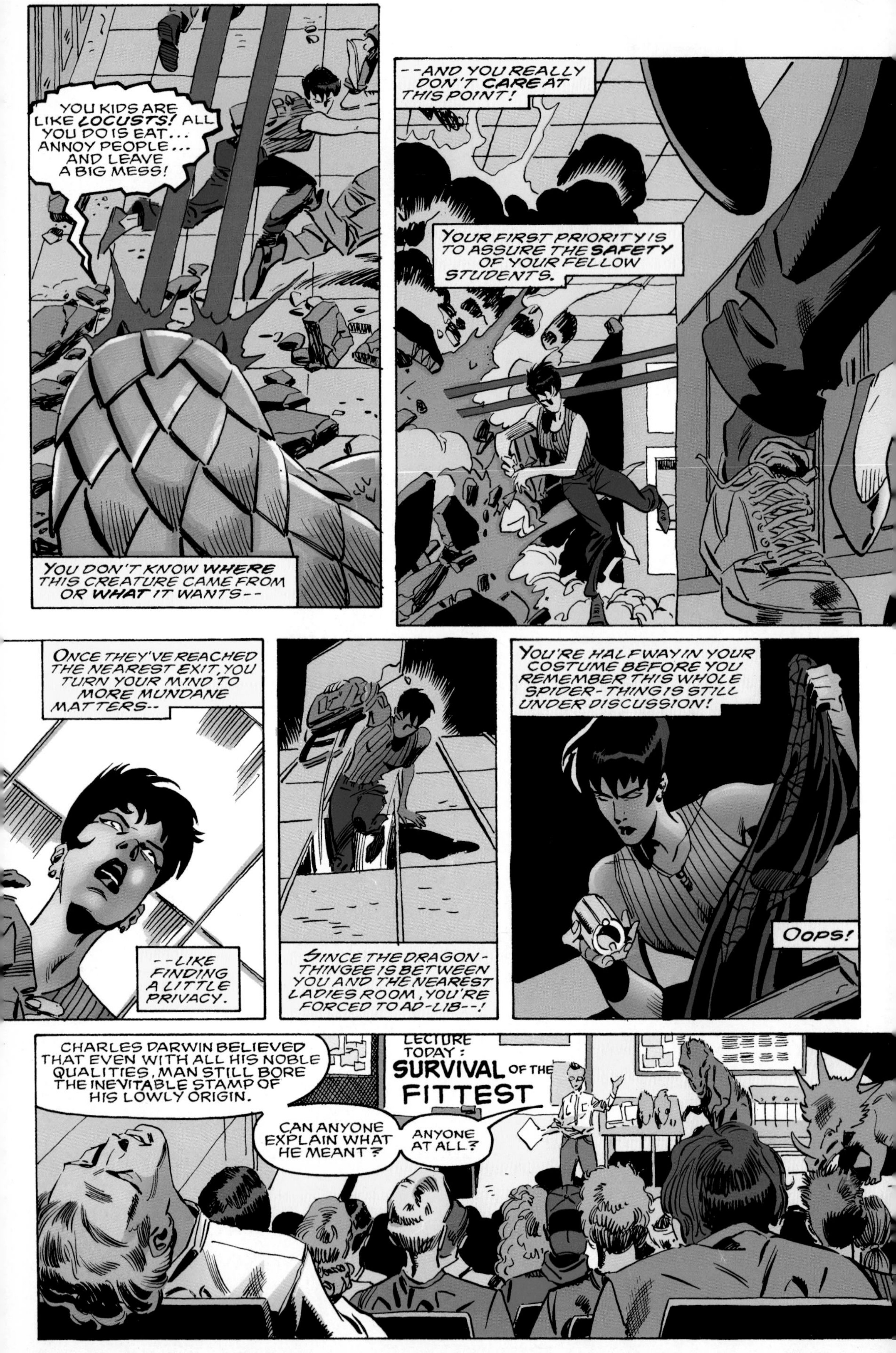
YOU KIDS ARE LIKE LOCUSTS! ALL YOU DO IS EAT... ANNOY PEOPLE... AND LEAVE A BIG MESS!
YOU DON'T KNOW WHERE THIS CREATURE CAME FROM OR WHAT IT WANTS--
--AND YOU REALLY DON'T CARE AT THIS POINT!
YOUR FIRST PRIORITY IS TO ASSURE THE SAFETY OF YOUR FELLOW STUDENTS.
ONCE THEY'VE REACHED THE NEAREST EXIT, YOU TURN YOUR MIND TO MORE MUNDANE MATTERS--
--LIKE FINDING A LITTLE PRIVACY.
SINCE THE DRAGON-THINGEE IS BETWEEN YOU AND THE NEAREST LADIES ROOM, YOU'RE FORCED TO AD-LIB--!
YOU'RE HALFWAY IN YOUR COSTUME BEFORE YOU REMEMBER THIS WHOLE SPIDER-THING IS STILL UNDER DISCUSSION!
OOPS!
CHARLES DARWIN BELIEVED THAT EVEN WITH ALL HIS NOBLE QUALITIES, MAN STILL BORE THE INEVITABLE STAMP OF HIS LOWLY ORIGIN.
LECTURE TODAY: SURVIVAL OF THE FITTEST
CAN ANYONE EXPLAIN WHAT HE MEANT?
ANYONE AT ALL?

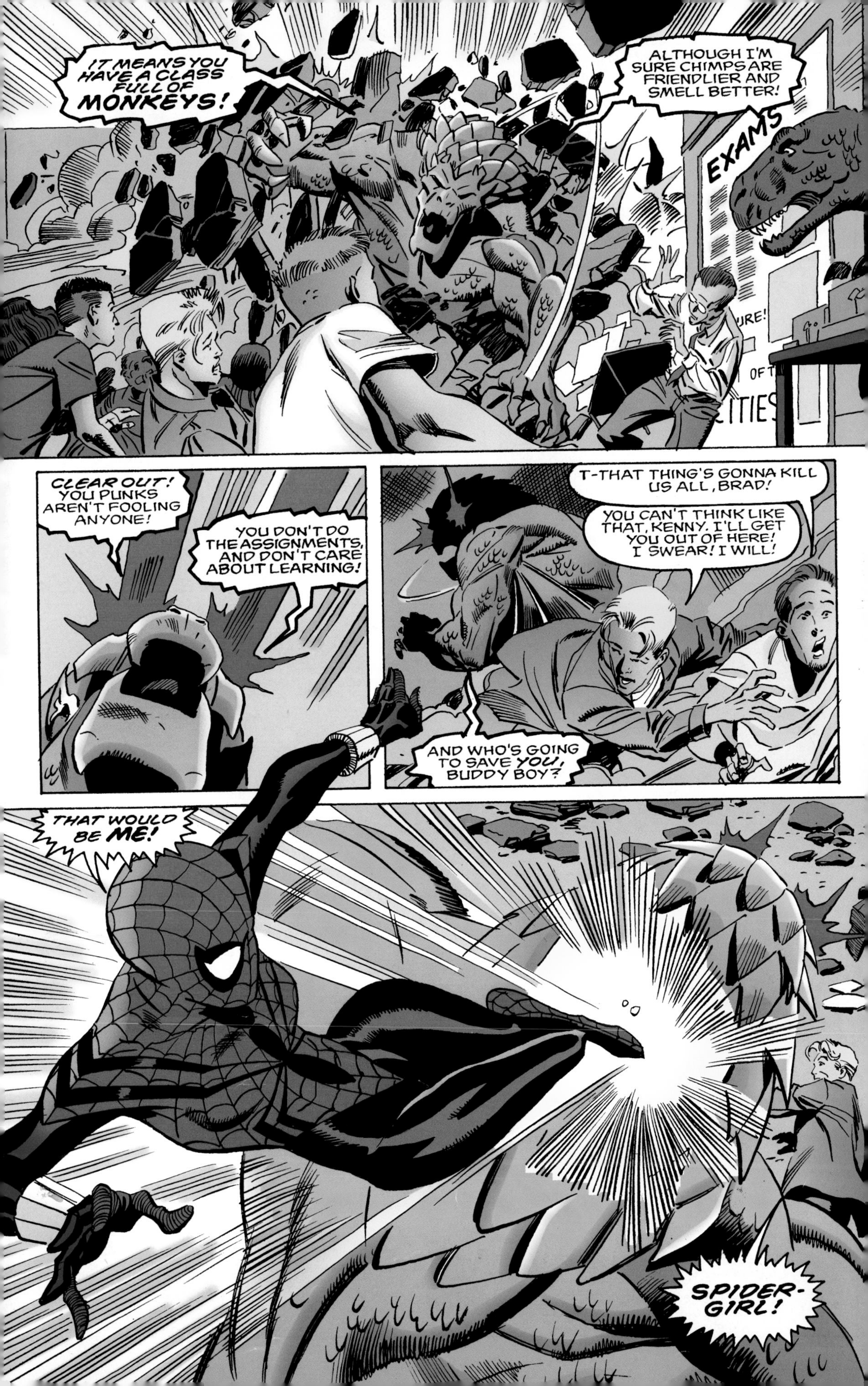
IT MEANS YOU HAVE A CLASS FULL OF MONKEYS!
ALTHOUGH I'M SURE CHIMPS ARE FRIENDLIER AND SMELL BETTER!
EXAMS
CLEAR OUT! YOU PUNKS AREN'T FOOLING ANYONE!
YOU DON'T DO THE ASSIGNMENTS, AND DON'T CARE ABOUT LEARNING!
T-THAT THING'S GONNA KILL US ALL, BRAD!
YOU CAN'T THINK LIKE THAT, KENNY. I'LL GET YOU OUT OF HERE! I SWEAR! I WILL!
AND WHO'S GOING TO SAVE YOU, BUDDY BOY?
THAT WOULD BE ME!
SPIDER-GIRL!

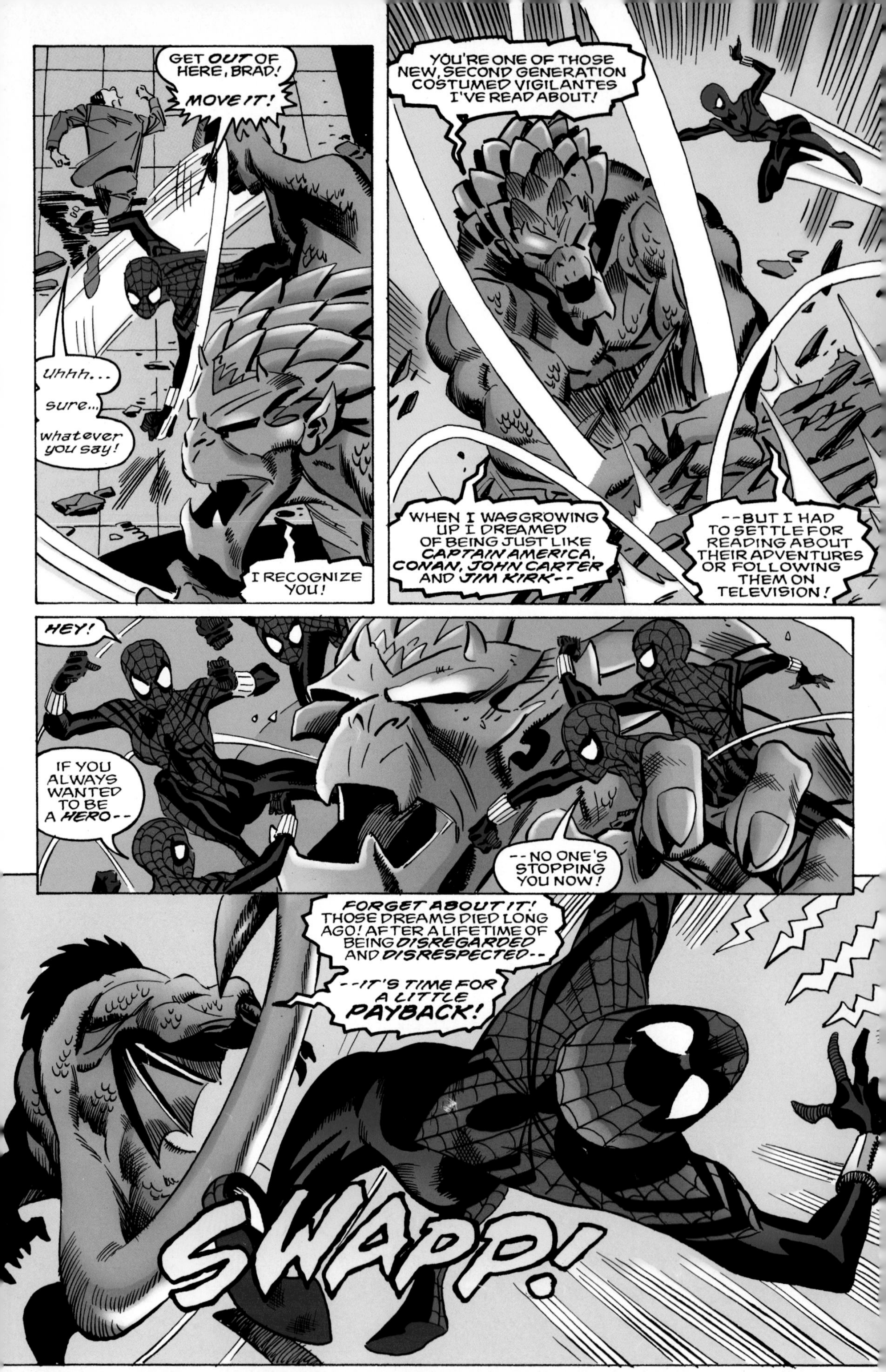
GET OUT OF HERE, BRAD! MOVE IT!
uhhh... sure... whatever you say!
I RECOGNIZE YOU!
YOU'RE ONE OF THOSE NEW, SECOND GENERATION COSTUMED VIGILANTES I'VE READ ABOUT!
WHEN I WAS GROWING UP I DREAMED OF BEING JUST LIKE CAPTAIN AMERICA, CONAN, JOHN CARTER AND JIM KIRK--
--BUT I HAD TO SETTLE FOR READING ABOUT THEIR ADVENTURES OR FOLLOWING THEM ON TELEVISION!
HEY!
IF YOU ALWAYS WANTED TO BE A HERO--
--NO ONE'S STOPPING YOU NOW!
FORGET ABOUT IT! THOSE DREAMS DIED LONG AGO! AFTER A LIFETIME OF BEING DISREGARDED AND DISRESPECTED--
--IT'S TIME FOR A LITTLE PAYBACK!
SWAPP!

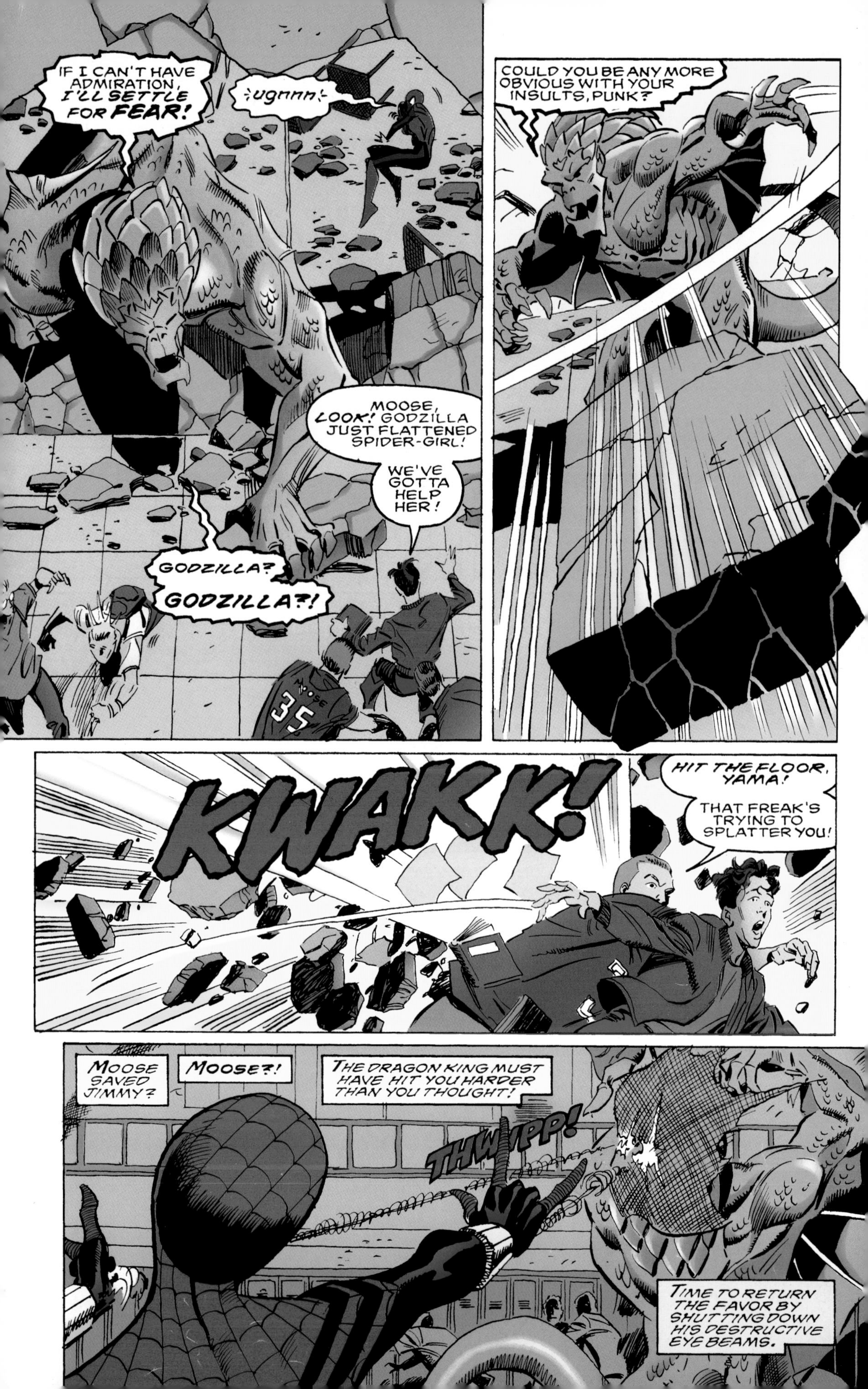
IF I CAN'T HAVE ADMIRATION, I'LL SETTLE FOR FEAR!
-ugnnn!-
MOOSE, LOOK! GODZILLA JUST FLATTENED SPIDER-GIRL!
WE'VE GOTTA HELP HER!
GODZILLA? GODZILLA?!
MOOSE
35
COULD YOU BE ANY MORE OBVIOUS WITH YOUR INSULTS, PUNK?
KWAKK!
HIT THE FLOOR, YAMA!
THAT FREAK'S TRYING TO SPLATTER YOU!
MOOSE SAVED JIMMY?
MOOSE?!
THE DRAGON KING MUST HAVE HIT YOU HARDER THAN YOU THOUGHT!
THWIPP!
TIME TO RETURN THE FAVOR BY SHUTTING DOWN HIS DESTRUCTIVE EYE BEAMS.

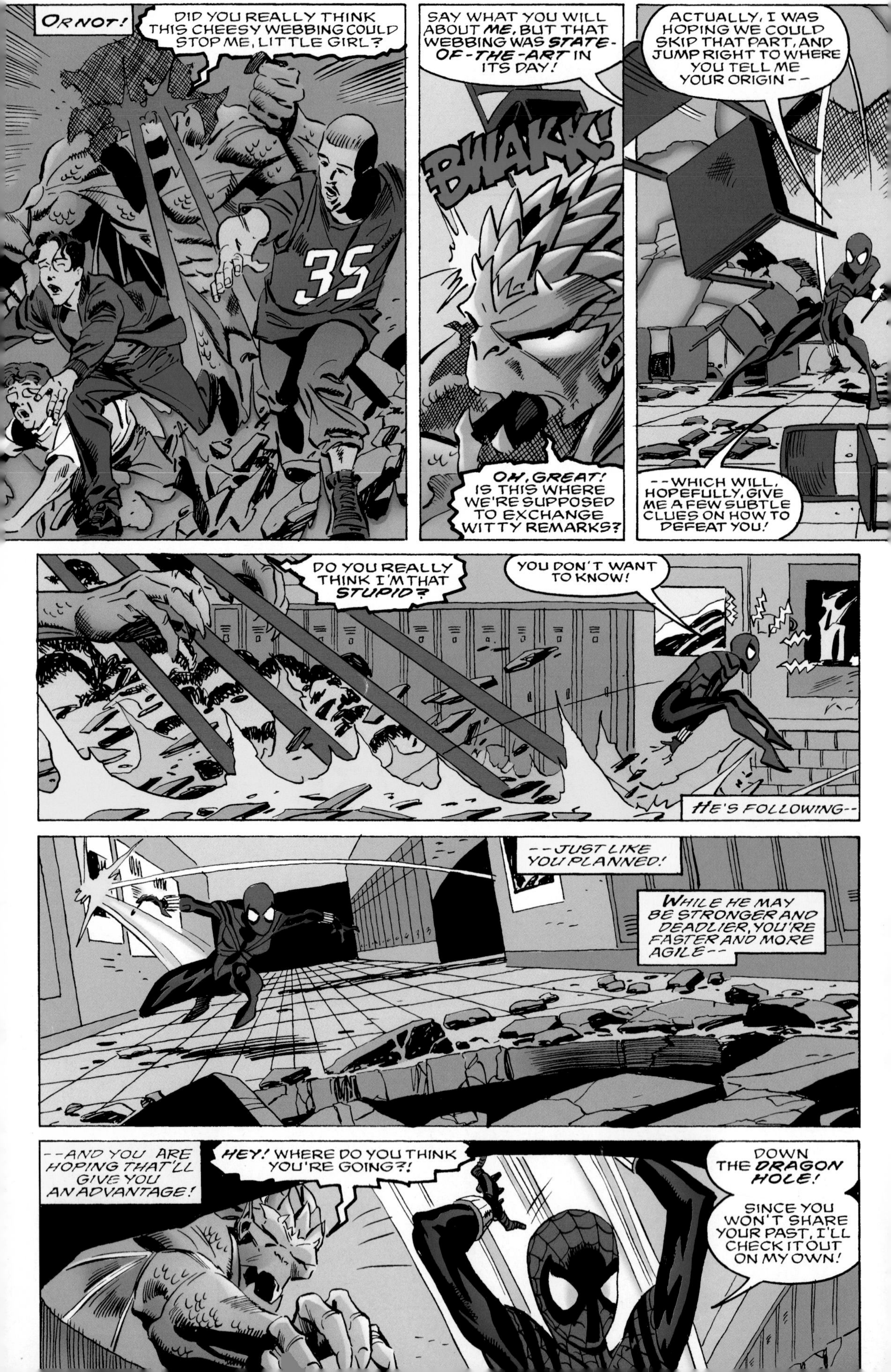
OR NOT!
DID YOU REALLY THINK THIS CHEESY WEBBING COULD STOP ME, LITTLE GIRL?
SAY WHAT YOU WILL ABOUT ME, BUT THAT WEBBING WAS STATE-OF-THE-ART IN ITS DAY!
BWAKK!
OH, GREAT! IS THIS WHERE WE'RE SUPPOSED TO EXCHANGE WITTY REMARKS?
ACTUALLY, I WAS HOPING WE COULD SKIP THAT PART, AND JUMP RIGHT TO WHERE YOU TELL ME YOUR ORIGIN--
--WHICH WILL, HOPEFULLY, GIVE ME A FEW SUBTLE CLUES ON HOW TO DEFEAT YOU!
DO YOU REALLY THINK I'M THAT STUPID?
YOU DON'T WANT TO KNOW!
HE'S FOLLOWING--
--JUST LIKE YOU PLANNED!
WHILE HE MAY BE STRONGER AND DEADLIER, YOU'RE FASTER AND MORE AGILE--
--AND YOU ARE HOPING THAT'LL GIVE YOU AN ADVANTAGE!
HEY! WHERE DO YOU THINK YOU'RE GOING?!
DOWN THE DRAGON HOLE!
SINCE YOU WON'T SHARE YOUR PAST, I'LL CHECK IT OUT ON MY OWN!

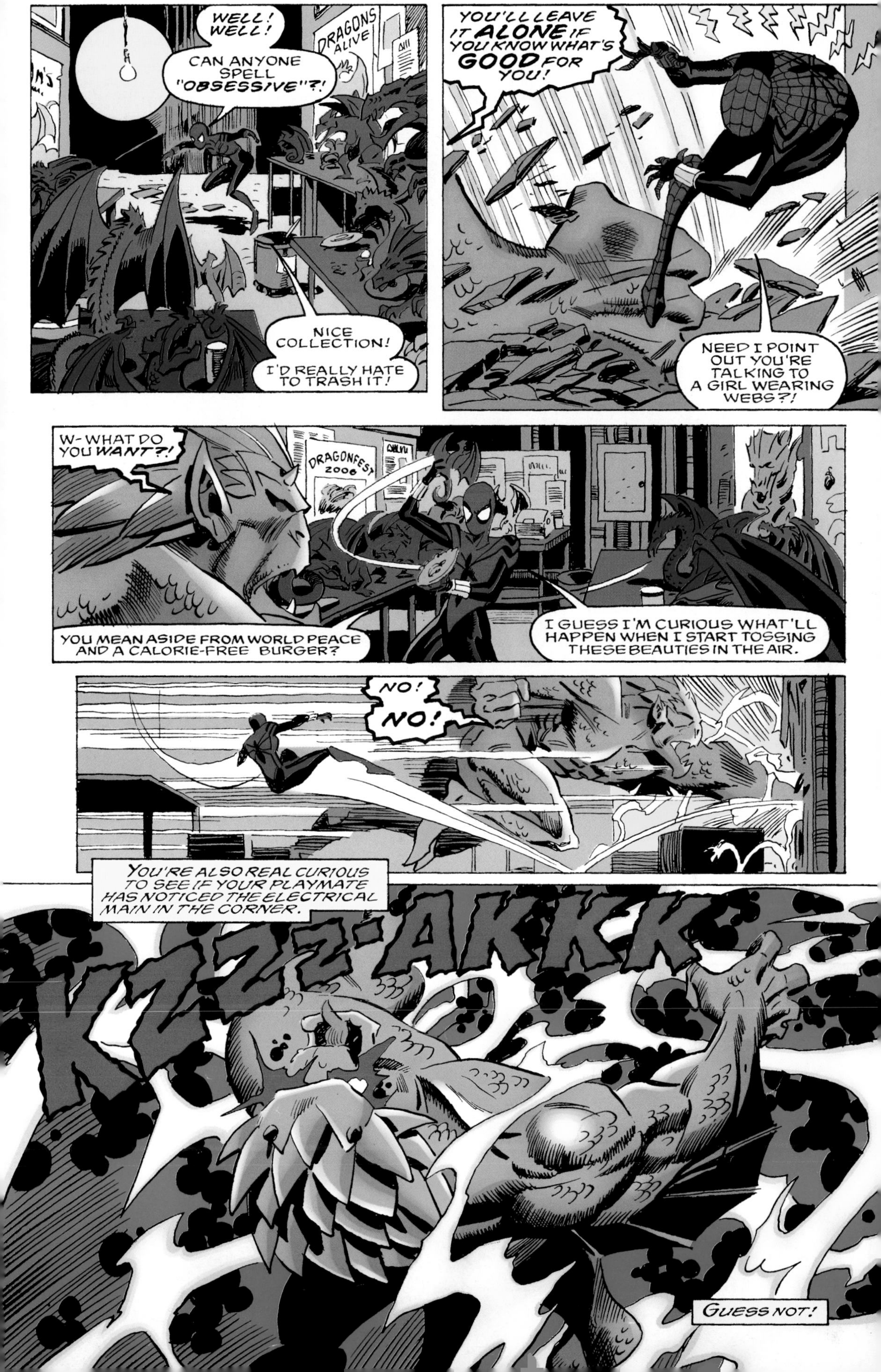

WELL! WELL!
CAN ANYONE SPELL "OBSESSIVE"?!
DRAGONS ALIVE
NICE COLLECTION!
I'D REALLY HATE TO TRASH IT!
YOU'LL LEAVE IT ALONE IF YOU KNOW WHAT'S GOOD FOR YOU!
NEED I POINT OUT YOU'RE TALKING TO A GIRL WEARING WEBS?!
W-WHAT DO YOU WANT?!
DRAGONFEST 2006
YOU MEAN ASIDE FROM WORLD PEACE AND A CALORIE-FREE BURGER?
I GUESS I'M CURIOUS WHAT'LL HAPPEN WHEN I START TOSSING THESE BEAUTIES IN THE AIR.
NO! NO!
YOU'RE ALSO REAL CURIOUS TO SEE IF YOUR PLAYMATE HAS NOTICED THE ELECTRICAL MAIN IN THE CORNER.
KZZZ-AKKK
GUESS NOT!

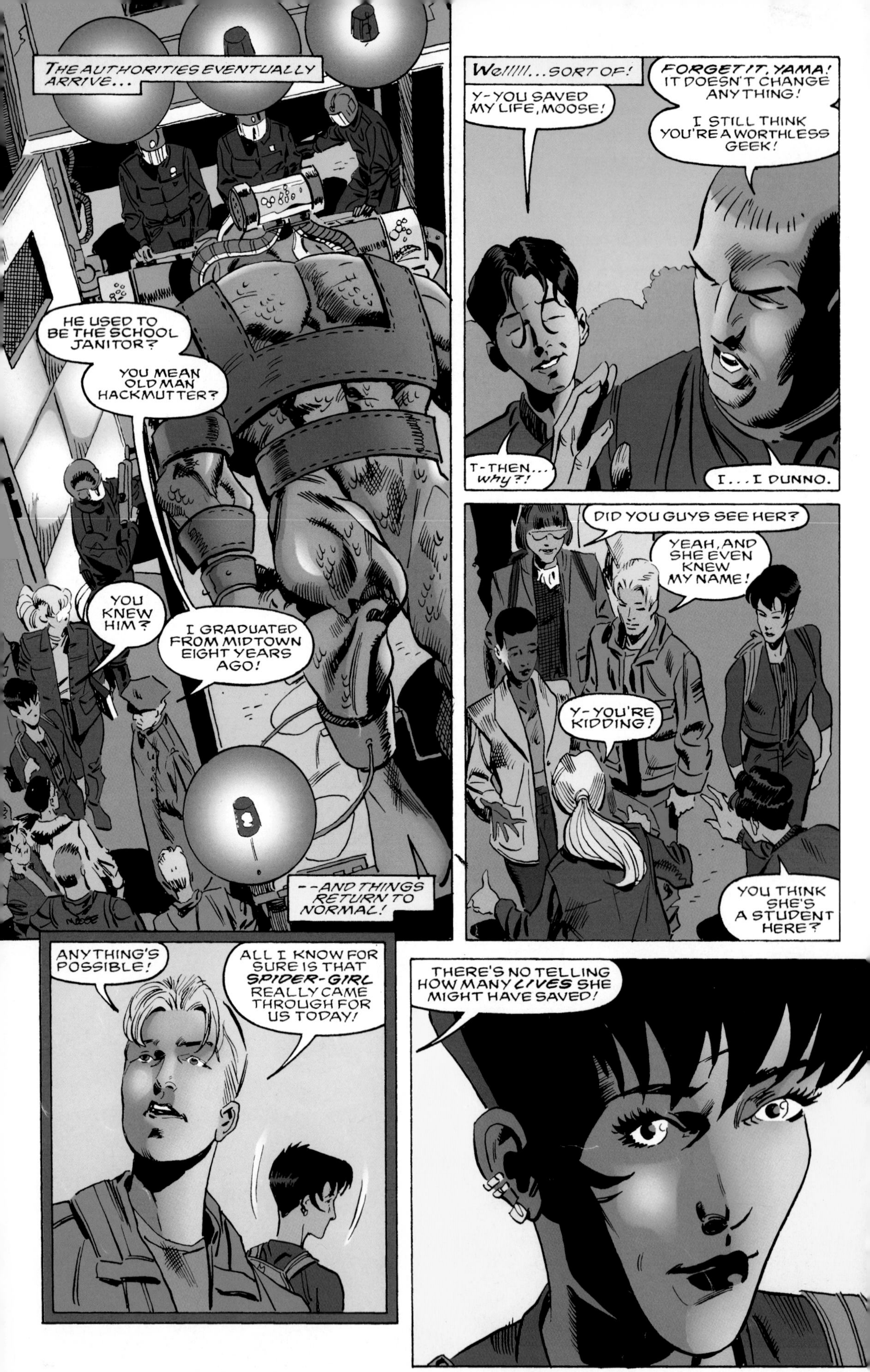
THE AUTHORITIES EVENTUALLY ARRIVE...
HE USED TO BE THE SCHOOL JANITOR?
YOU MEAN OLD MAN HACKMUTTER?
YOU KNEW HIM?
I GRADUATED FROM MIDTOWN EIGHT YEARS AGO!
--AND THINGS RETURN TO NORMAL!
Welllll... SORT OF!
Y-YOU SAVED MY LIFE, MOOSE!
FORGET IT, YAMA! IT DOESN'T CHANGE ANYTHING!
I STILL THINK YOU'RE A WORTHLESS GEEK!
T-THEN... why?!
I... I DUNNO.
DID YOU GUYS SEE HER?
YEAH, AND SHE EVEN KNEW MY NAME!
Y-YOU'RE KIDDING!
YOU THINK SHE'S A STUDENT HERE?
ANYTHING'S POSSIBLE!
ALL I KNOW FOR SURE IS THAT SPIDER-GIRL REALLY CAME THROUGH FOR US TODAY!
THERE'S NO TELLING HOW MANY LIVES SHE MIGHT HAVE SAVED!

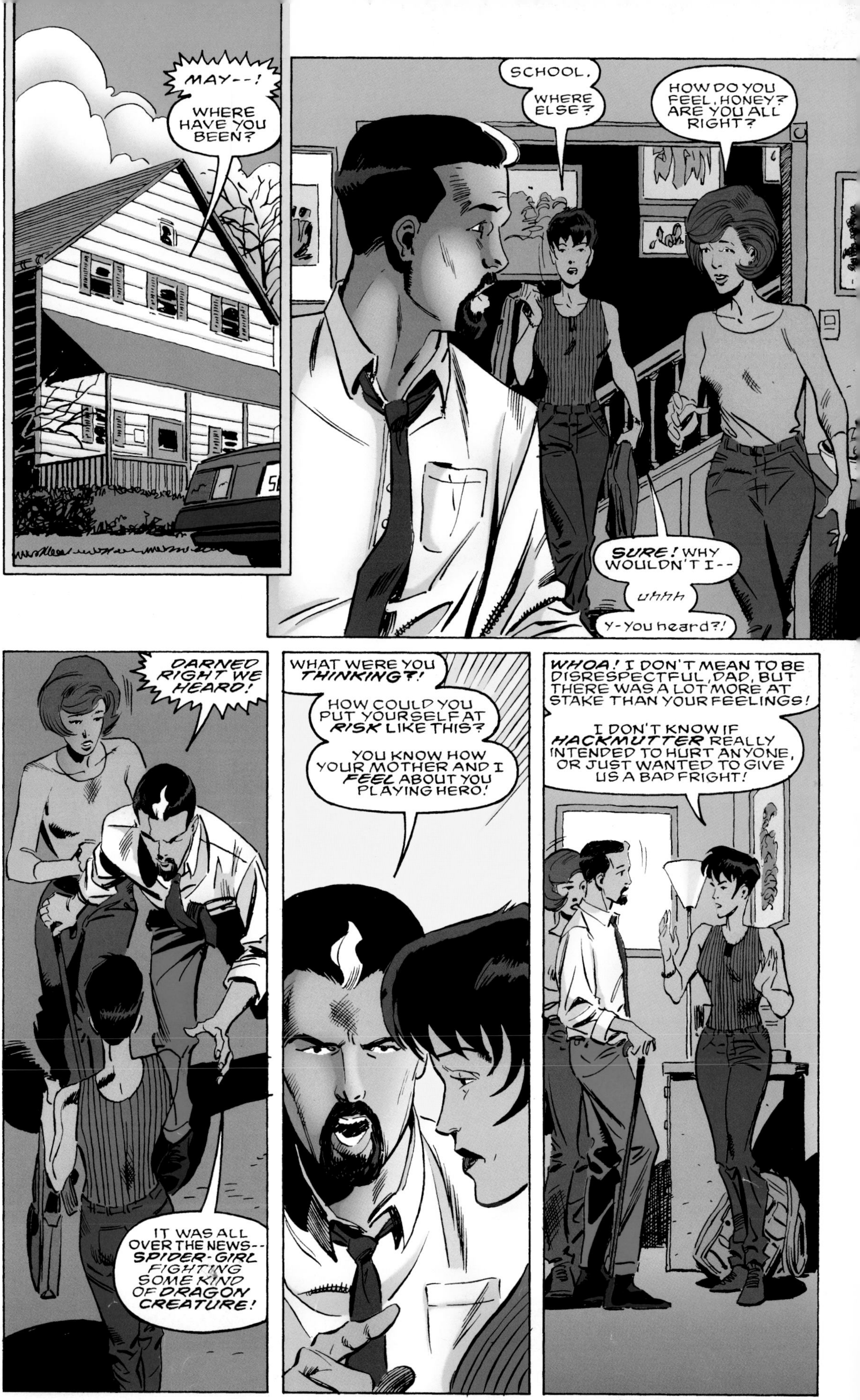
MAY--!
WHERE HAVE YOU BEEN?
SCHOOL,
WHERE ELSE?
HOW DO YOU FEEL, HONEY? ARE YOU ALL RIGHT?
SURE! WHY WOULDN'T I--
uhhh
Y-You heard?!
DARNED RIGHT WE HEARD!
IT WAS ALL OVER THE NEWS-- SPIDER-GIRL FIGHTING SOME KIND OF DRAGON CREATURE!
WHAT WERE YOU THINKING?!
HOW COULD YOU PUT YOURSELF AT RISK LIKE THIS?
YOU KNOW HOW YOUR MOTHER AND I FEEL ABOUT YOU PLAYING HERO!
WHOA! I DON'T MEAN TO BE DISRESPECTFUL, DAD, BUT THERE WAS A LOT MORE AT STAKE THAN YOUR FEELINGS!
I DON'T KNOW IF HACKMUTTER REALLY INTENDED TO HURT ANYONE, OR JUST WANTED TO GIVE US A BAD FRIGHT!

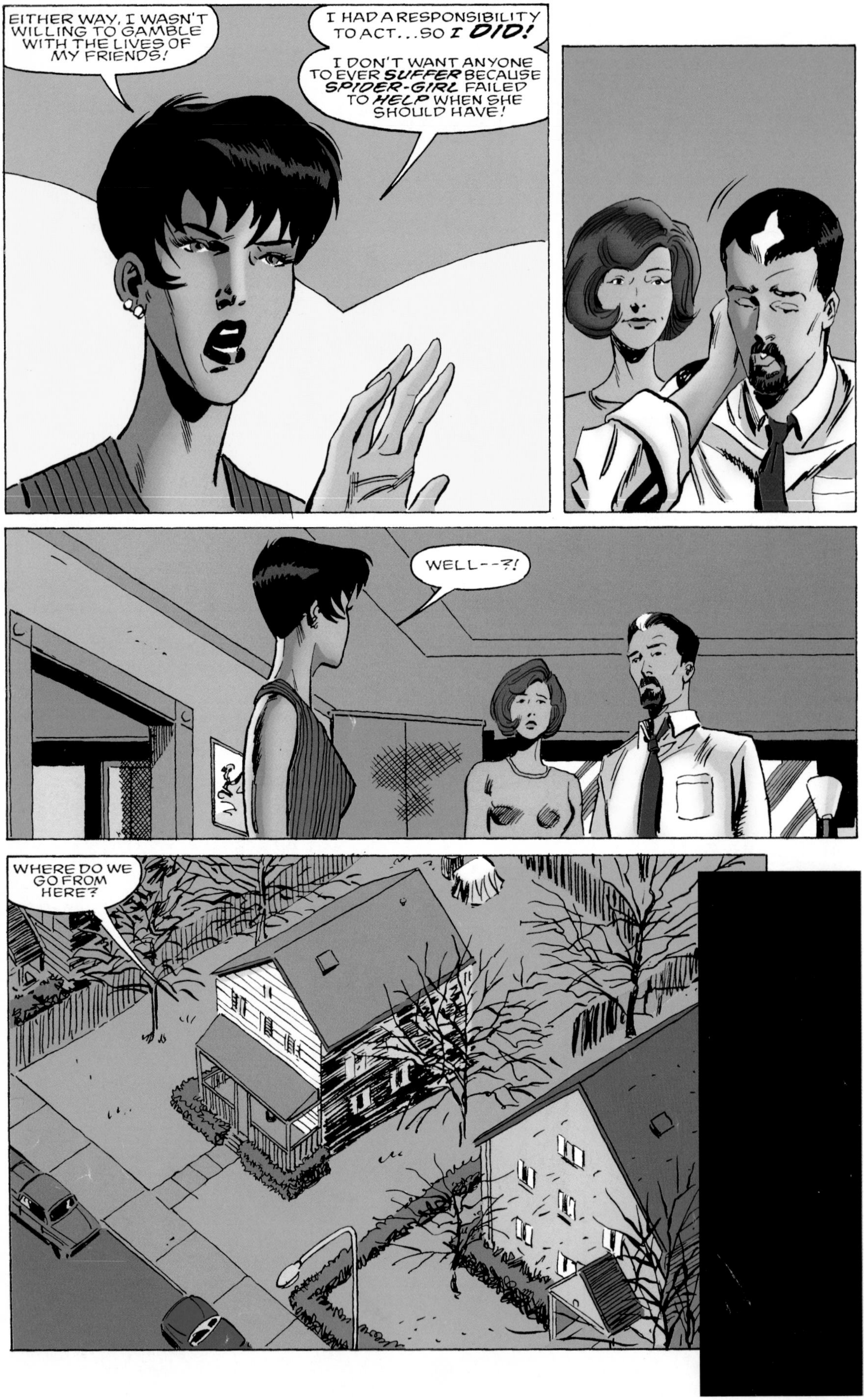
EITHER WAY, I WASN'T WILLING TO GAMBLE WITH THE LIVES OF MY FRIENDS!
I HAD A RESPONSIBILITY TO ACT... SO I **DID!**
I DON'T WANT ANYONE TO EVER **SUFFER** BECAUSE **SPIDER-GIRL** FAILED TO **HELP** WHEN SHE SHOULD HAVE!
WELL--?!
WHERE DO WE GO FROM HERE?

[redacted]